D0333147

4339501003098442772 6012

HAVE YOU SEEN WHO'S JUST MOVED IN NEXT DOOR TO US?

Colin McNaughton

WALKER BOOKS
AND SUBSIDIARIES
LONDON · BOSTON · SYDNEY

For May and Tom!

First published 1991 by
Walker Books Ltd, 87 Vauxhall Walk
London SE11 5HJ

This edition published 1993

Reprinted 1994 (twice), 1997, 1998, 1999, 2000

© 1991 Colin McNaughton

Printed in Hong Kong

British Library Cataloguing in Publication Data
A catalogue record for this book is
available from the British Library.

ISBN 0-7445-3043-1

We've a lovely bunch of people in our street;
    Yes, a nicer crowd you couldn't wish to meet.
But there's been an awful change –
    We've new neighbours; man, they're strange!
Have you seen who's just moved in
            Next door to us?

Let me introduce my friends, you will agree –
    Perfect neighbours, every one, as you will see.
But they'll be as shocked as me,
    As I'm certain you will be,
When they see who's just moved in
            Next door to us.

Say hello to Mister Thing;
Squirting, squelching, slithering.
(Has he seen who's just moved in
Next door to us?)

Meet the Dumptys – one's in bed;
    Took a tumble, cracked his head!
(Have they seen who's just moved in
    Next door to us?)

I'm afraid they get no thinner –
    They've a dozen eggs for dinner!
(Have they seen who's just moved in
    Next door to us?)

See the shop, it's just for pigs;
It sells plain and fancy wigs.
(Have they seen who's just moved in
Next door to us?)

And a school, it teaches birds
    To say rude and silly words.
    (Have they seen who's just moved in
    Next door to us?)

Something missing? Look no more.
   Tom will have it (twenty-four).
(Has he seen who's just moved in
   Next door to us?)

Under Tom (I swear it's true!)
   Are the local boys in blue.
(Have they seen who's just moved in
   Next door to us?)

And further down the road,
    Salute the Duke of York's abode.
(Has he seen who's just moved in
    Next door to us?)

An old lady with a broom,
  At number forty rents a room.
(Has she seen who's just moved in
  Next door to us?)

And living down below,
  We have Michelangelo.
(Has he seen who's just moved in
  Next door to us?)

Move five doors along:
    Say hello to Mister Kong.
(Has he seen who's just moved in
    Next door to us?)

Round the fountain in the park
    Swims a hammer-headed shark!
(Has it seen who's just moved in
    Next door to us?)

And piranhas, there's a school
    Cruising round the paddling pool.
(Have they seen who's just moved in
    Next door to us?)

Have you seen them yet, Mr Backwards?

!ON

See the creature, soft and rubbery,
   Hiding deep within the shrubbery.
(Has it seen who's just moved in
   Next door to us?)

And though the postman may complain,
   Here's where Tarzan lives with Jane.
(Have they seen who's just moved in
   Next door to us?)

Leather, denim, oil and grime –
    We've Hell's Angels (fifty-nine).
(Have they seen who's just moved in
    Next door to us?)

There's Mr Thread (it's true, I swear),
    When he's in, he isn't there!
(Has he seen who's just moved in
    Next door to us?)

And at number seven zero,
Meet a certain super hero.
(Has he seen who's just moved in
Next door to us?)

Though I know I shouldn't boast,
  This house is haunted by a ghost.
(Has she seen who's just moved in
  Next door to us?)

In the steeple lives a man,
　　He keeps the belfry spick and span.
(Has he seen who's just moved in
　　Next door to us?)

I've a hunch I know him well,
　　It's his face that rings a bell.
(Has he seen who's just moved in
　　Next door to us?)

In the graveyard by the church,
   Ghouls and ghosties limp and lurch.
(Have they seen who's just moved in
   Next door to us?)

Shoe shavers! Pass it on.

At eighty-three the window-lace
   Hides the folks from outer space.
(Have they seen who's just moved in
   Next door to us?)

And at number eighty-nine
   Lives my old friend Frankenstein.
(Has he seen who's just moved in
   Next door to us?)

Avast there, ninety-four!
    Abdul's pirates are ashore!
(Have they seen who's just moved in
    Next door to us?)

At one hundred an old fella
    With horns, lives in the cellar.
(Has he seen who's just moved in
    Next door to us?)

There's a man above the dairy;
  When the moon shines he gets hairy!
(Has he seen who's just moved in
  Next door to us?)

I think we'll leave this miscellanea
And return to Transylvania –
'Cause have you seen who's just moved in
Next door to us?

Well, I hope you're feeling strong,
   Because now it won't be long
Till you see who's just moved in
   Next door to us.

Yes, the time has come, I feel;
   I am ready to reveal
Who, or what, has just moved in
   Next door to us.

Lift the flaps and take a look;
   You'll see why I wrote this book…

SONG
BIRDS
GOING
CHEAP

UNUSUAL
PETS Pet Shop CATS
DOGS
MICE

FAT PIG INC
FUNNY MONEY

CASH·LOANS

New neighbours!
Pass it on.

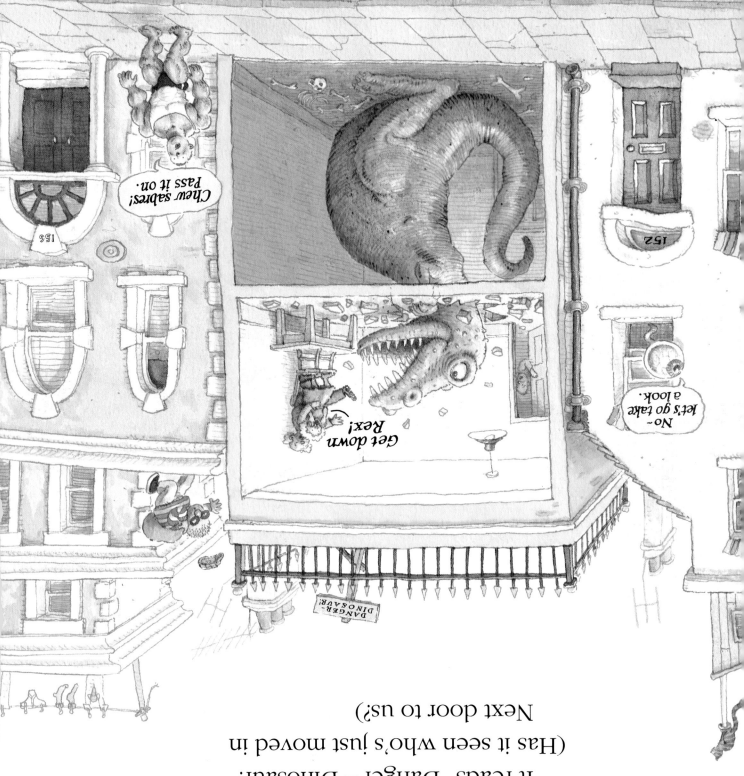

There is a sign at one five four;
It reads "Danger – Dinosaur!"
(Has it seen who's just moved in
Next door to us?)